This Boxer Books paperback belongs to

.. DARREN GILLIES OCT 2015 ..

HAPPY BIRTHDAY

DARREN

Sunny ~ Sean.

xxx

www.boxerbooks.com

The IFMGA(International Federation of Mountain Guides Associations) is made up of 22 national associations from North and South America, Asia and Europe. Mark Seaton is one of about 6,000 certified IFMGA guides who look after guests on mountains all over the world. IFMGA certified mountain guides like Mark Seaton understand the mountains and can teach others to enjoy these wonderful environments in safety. The IFMGA is a non-profit organisation that supports mountain guide training programs for young people in developing countries such as Bolivia, Ecuador, Peru, Nepal, and Tibet.

For more information go to
www.ifmga.info

MARK
THE MOUNTAIN GUIDE

™

BOXER BOOKS

WRITTEN BY
MARK SEATON

ILLUSTRATED BY
GRAHAM PHILPOT

Sorbet Summit

Prickly Ridge

Sorbet Glacier

Grumpy
Gorge
Bridge

Grumpy
Gorge

Ice Cream Glacier

Ralph Raven Rescue

Marmot
Mountaineering
School

A message from
Sir Chris Bonington

Mountains are exciting and inspiring.
We look up to them; fly over them;
ski on them. But the most thrilling way
to experience a mountain is to climb one.
People have been climbing mountains for
hundreds of years, learning great skills and
seeing extraordinary landscapes that few
people ever get to see.

Experts like Mark the Mountain Guide really
do exist. They are there to help you learn to
climb safely. I started climbing very young, and
the more I learned, the better I could climb.
Eventually I climbed the highest mountain
in the world, Mount Everest. Perhaps one day
you will, too. For now, have fun with Mark
and his friends!

Chris Bonington

It was a beautiful morning in High Alps,
when suddenly,

Kaboom!

The little marmot mountaineers woke up with a start.
Mark the Mountain Guide rushed outside the mountain
hut, followed by the little mountaineers.
"Everyone, stay where you are!" shouted Mark.
An enormous avalanche had blocked Mark's mountain path.
The little mountaineers, students of
the Marmot Mountaineering School, watched as
heaps of icy snow settled down nearby.

Mark the Mountain Guide made sure all his climbers were safe.

He called their names from his checklist.

"Eddy?" he called.

"Epic!" said Eddy in wonderment.

"Leo?"

"Here," Leo said, shaking his head at the near disaster.

"Marmots?"

"One! Two! Three! Whee!"

said the little marmots all together. They had been climbing since they were babies. They loved the mountains.

"We'll have to get down to the village another way,"
said Mark as he surveyed the map. "We'll need to go
through Grumpy Gorge, across the Sorbet Glacier,
and then over the Applestrudelhorn."

"The Applestrudelhorn!" cried the marmots.

They couldn't help being excited.

"I don't like the sound of that," said Leo.

"Sounds rather tasty to me," Eddy said.

Then they all packed their rucksacks and checked

their equipment carefully before setting off.

Mark led them first to Grumpy Gorge.

From way off they could hear the sound of a marmot whistling. It was sending them a signal.

"What is it saying?" Eddy asked the marmots.

The little marmots listened carefully.

"The bridge . . . has . . . collapsed!" they exclaimed.

"I knew it!" said Leo.

"The bridge has collapsed, the bridge has collapsed," a little marmot repeated. Then he whistled back a "thank you" to the marmot who had warned them.

"Okay, listen everyone," said Mark,
pulling a climbing rope out of his bag
and tying a wide slipknot with one end.
"This is what we're going to do."
With a few flicks of his wrist, Mark threw
the rope across Grumpy Gorge and lassoed
a spike of rock on the other side.

Mark tied his end of the rope around
a big, sturdy rock and pulled it tight.
"We're going to slide across this rope,"
Mark announced.
"Epic!" said Eddy.
"A challenge," said Leo, "but I think we
can all handle it! Eddy, you go first!"

Eddy was proud to be first.
The little marmots scrambled onto Eddy
and secured themselves with
a carabiner each.

"One! Two! Three! Whee!"
the marmots said together as Eddy slid across
the open gorge on Mark's sturdy rope.

Mark helped Leo, making sure he was secured with rope
and carabiners. Then they too slid safely across.

"We'd better keep moving," Mark said.

"We'll need to travel as far as we can before dark."

The afternoon sun twinkled on the ice as the mountaineers approached Sorbet Glacier. "Glaciers are made of ice and have big cracks in them called crevasses," Mark explained as he pulled a rope out of his rucksack.

"Sometimes the crevasses are hidden by snow," said Leo.

"Right," replied Mark, "so we must be very careful."

"Don't worry, team," Mark said. "We're going to tie ourselves to my rope. I'll lead us over a safe path so that no one falls down a crevasse."

"One!

　　Two!

　　　Three!"

The marmots showed Eddy and Leo how they could tie secure knots in the rope.

The mountaineers carefully trekked across
Sorbet Glacier, making sure the rope was not
too loose or too tight between them.

"Epic," whispered Eddy.
The sun was disappearing behind High Alps
and the temperature was falling fast.

"It's getting dark," said Mark. "We'll need to spend
the night here and go on in the morning."
"Where will we sleep?" asked Leo.
"We're going to build ourselves a home
for the night," said Mark.
"Epic!" said Eddy once again.

Mark gave each mountaineer a task.

Eddy used a snow saw to cut blocks of snow.

Leo helped carry the snow blocks, and Mark showed
them how to build an igloo.

Meanwhile, the little marmots melted snow
for drinking water and to use for cooking dinner.

Mark called Mary Marmot at the Marmot Mountaineering School
base camp on his mobile phone to tell her everyone was safe.

At last the tired mountaineers looked up
at the stars before settling into their igloo.
The night sky was filled with stars, and they
could clearly see many constellations.
For once, even Eddy was speechless.

The next morning, everyone woke up smiling.
"Applestrudelhorn!" said Mark as he pointed out
the majestic mountain.
"You little guys have climbed the Applestrudelhorn
before, right?" Leo asked the marmots.

"One!

　　Two!

　　　　Three!

Not me!" said all three little marmots together.

"Disaster," said Eddy.

"Can they handle it?" asked Leo.

"Don't worry, mountaineers," said Mark.

"I'll show you what to do."

Following Mark's instructions, and using their crampons, carabiners, and ropes, the mountaineers carefully inched their way up Applestrudelhorn. One step at a time, they made it to the top of the mountain. As they stood on the summit, the view was breathtaking.

Everything below them looked so small.

In the distance, they could see the tiny village of High Alp.

Mark congratulated them. "Well done, mountaineers!"

"One!

    Two!

        Three!

Yippee!" said the little marmots all together.

"Yippee," said Eddy, joining in. "But, Mark, how do we get down?"

Mark began to pull something out of his rucksack.

"Not another rope?" asked Leo.

"No," said Mark, "no more climbing – just flying!"

Eddy and the little mountaineers wriggled with excitement.

Mark gave each of them a parachute and they all buckled in carefully.

"Ready?" asked Mark. "Then follow me!"

The flying mountaineers floated down across the valley to the Marmot Mountaineering School base camp, where Mary Marmot would be waiting for them with mugs of delicious hot chocolate.

"Wait a minute," said Mark.

"Where's Eddy?"

Suddenly they heard an enormous

THUMP!

Eddy had landed on Mary's roof!
"Just in time for a mug of hot
chocolate, Eddy!" said Mary.
"Epic!" Eddy exclaimed.

The mountaineers congratulated themselves
on a great climbing adventure.

"It was EPIC!" said Eddy.

"What was it?" asked Mark.

"It was EPIC!" they all said together,
and laughed out loud.

AVALANCHE

Mountains are beautiful, but they can also be dangerous. One of the biggest dangers is an avalanche.

An avalanche is a mass of snow falling down a mountainside. Avalanches come in all shapes and sizes, from little ones, just big enough to cover a marmot, to huge ones that block entire paths as the avalanche does in our story.

There are specially trained people living in the mountains called avalanche forecasters. They can tell you when it is too dangerous to go into the mountains. Mountain guides like Mark are trained as avalanche forecasters.

WHAT CAUSES AN AVALANCHE?

Snow causes an avalanche – lots and lots of snow in layers! When the top layers become too heavy to stick to the layers of snow underneath, they slide off. This can happen if there is a big snowstorm, or when the snow gets warm, as it does in springtime.

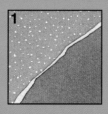

Always check the weather and avalanche forecast before going into the mountains!

WHAT IS A CARABINER?

A carabiner is a metal ring with a springy opener called a 'gate'. There are two types:

A snap link carabiner and a locking carabiner. Climbers use this kind for all types of climbing situations. A climber may carry about 24 of these on a climb.

Climbers call carabiners 'crabs' or 'biners' (say as 'bean-ers').

SNAP LINK CARABINER
Sometimes two of these are joined together to form a 'quickdraw'. Quickdraws are used to clip the rope to a safety device the climber has put into the rock face.

LOCKING CARABINER
It has a screw-down gate so that it cannot come open easily. This type is used to tie the climber safely to an anchor point.

Eddy always carries spare carabiners in case the student climbers lose some of their own!

REALLY IMPORTANT ROPE

Climbing rope is a very important part of the climber's kit. It is used to tie climbers together, to hang from, slide down or climb up, and also to get across gaps like Grumpy Gorge.

Climbing rope is made of nylon and acts a bit like elastic that is not very stretchy. If you fall, the rope will stretch a bit and put less stress on you and the anchor in the rock face holding the rope. Eddy says he would like it to be a bit more stretchy so he can bounce! Mark does not think this is very funny.

Climbing rope looks like this if you unravel it.

Climbers use a rope about this thick. It does not seem strong enough to hold a grown-up, does it?

 After a climb, mountain climbers always take great care to coil up their ropes properly and hang them up on hooks so they do not get tangled or dirty before they're needed again!

If you want to be a mountaineer like Mark the Mountain Guide, you will have to learn how to tie knots. Here are two knots for you to try yourself. You might find it easier if you follow the pictures carefully and work on the floor or a table.

FIGURE EIGHT

1
Make a loop that looks like this one.

2
Pass the looped end over.

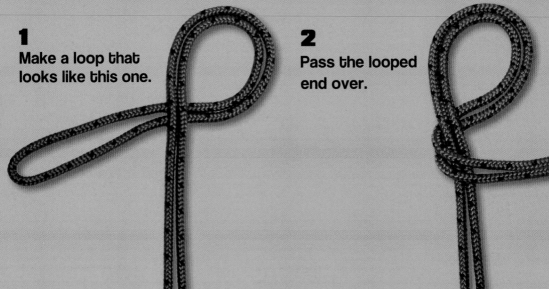

3
Push the looped end up through the large loop.

4
Put the loop into a carabiner and close the gate.

CLOVE HITCH

You will need to use a carabiner with this one, too. Note where the rope crosses over and under itself.

1

Make two loops exactly like this.

2

Lay the left-hand loop on top of the right-hand loop, like this. Then carefully pick them up with one hand so that they stay together.

3

gate ➜

Put the loops into a carabiner and close the gate.

4

You can tighten the loops by pulling the ends of the rope.

BE PREPARED!

Here is Mark the Mountain Guide properly kitted up to climb a snowy mountain.

Helmet
Very important to protect Mark's head from falling rocks or bangs against the rock face.

Snow suit
Wind- and snow-proof jacket and trousers. Thin layers underneath keep Mark warm and dry.

Harness
This is where Mark hangs all his climbing equipment such as carabiners and quickdraws.

Ice axe
This helps Mark climb up snow and ice.

Mountain boots
Insulated to keep Mark's feet warm, and shockproof to protect his feet against rough ground.

Rope
Used to tie Mark and his friends together or to attach to the rock face.

Crampons
These spikes fit onto Mark's boots and help him grip into snow and ice.

MARK'S RUCKSACK

Whistle

First aid pack

Map and compass

Water bottle

Food if Mark is climbing all day

Warm sweater or fleece

Waterproof trousers

Warm hat

Headlamp: leaves Mark's hands free

Mountaineers always fill in a Route Card when they go into the mountains. This card tells everyone where they are going and what time they are expected to return. If they are late, someone can go and help them!

MOUNTAINOUS FACT

WHAT IS A MOUNTAIN?

A mountain is steep sided land, rising more than 600 metres high. Anything less than this is just a hill!

HOW ARE MOUNTAINS MADE?

Our planet Earth is covered with a layer of rock called the crust. This crust is not one big sheet. It is made up of pieces like a jigsaw puzzle. These pieces move very, very slowly, and when they push against each other some of the crust is forced upwards. Over millions of years of pushing, this part of the crust is pushed so high it becomes a mountain range. Other mountains, such as Mauna Kea, are formed when volcanoes erupt and the hot lava hardens into peaks.

mountain range

crust

crust

The highest mountain on land is Mount Everest in the Himalayas. It is 8,863 metres high.

The highest mountain on Earth is Mauna Kea. It is in the Pacific Ocean and is 10,205 metres high. The top pokes out of the sea and is an island in Hawaii!

WHY ARE THE STARS SO BRIGHT IN THE MOUNTAINS?

When Mark and friends stayed overnight on the mountain, the stars looked bright and clear. This is because there is no other light up in the mountains to interfere with the view. Down in the valley, lights from street lamps, roads, and houses give off a glow of light which gets in the way of the view and makes it harder to see the stars.

OW TO MAKE AN IGLOO

The mountaineers had to make a shelter for the night to keep everyone warm and dry. This is how to make an igloo.

STEP 1 Cut blocks from very hard, dry snow with a large knife or special snow saw.

STEP 2 Stand in the hole you made when you cut the blocks and make a circle with your blocks. Make sure they fit together tightly.

STEP 3 Keep building up the blocks, shaping them as you go, so the sides slope inwards. Cut a hole under the wall to the outside. This is called a 'cold sink'.

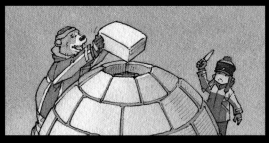

STEP 4 Put the last block on top. It must be bigger than the hole. From inside, cut it to fit.

STEP 5 It is very important to cut air holes in the sides of the igloo to make sure you have fresh air to breathe.

It gets very warm inside an igloo, even though it may be freezing and windy outside!

AVALANCHE
A large amount of snow that falls down a mountainside.

CARABINER
A metal ring with a spring-loaded opener used to connect rope to an anchor point or two ropes together.

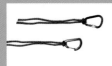

CRAMPONS
Spikes which are attached to the bottom of mountain boots and help climbers grip into snow and ice.

CREVASSES
Cracks in a glacier. They can be very dangerous if they are deep or hidden by snow.

GLACIER
A river of ice found high up the mountain. Glaciers move very slowly down the mountain.

GORGE
A deep narrow valley.

IGLOO
A house made from blocks of snow.

LASSO
Rope with a loop at the end to catch hold of something.

MARMOT
Large rodent (related to mice and squirrels) that lives in mountainous areas. Marmots call to each other with loud whistles.

MOUNTAIN GUIDE
Expert mountaineer who leads people up and down the mountain safely.

MOUNTAIN HUT
A place where mountaineers can stop and rest for the night and eat on their way up or down the mountain.

MOUNTAINEER
A person who climbs mountains.

SLIPKNOT
A knot that tightens when one end is pulled.

SUMMIT
Top or peak of a mountain.

First published in hardback in Great Britain in 2008 by Boxer Books Limited.
First published in paperback in Great Britain in 2011 by Boxer Books Limited.
www.boxerbooks.com

Mark The Mountain Guide copyright © 2008 Mark Seaton and Sam Williams
Text copyright © 2008 Mark Seaton
Illustrations copyright © 2008 Graham Philpot

The rights of Mark Seaton and Sam Williams to be identified
as the authors and Graham Philpot as the illustrator of this work have been
asserted by them in accordance with the Copyright, Designs and Patents Act, 1988.

ISBN 978-1-907-967-09-2

Printed in China

All of our papers are sourced from managed forests and renewable resources.